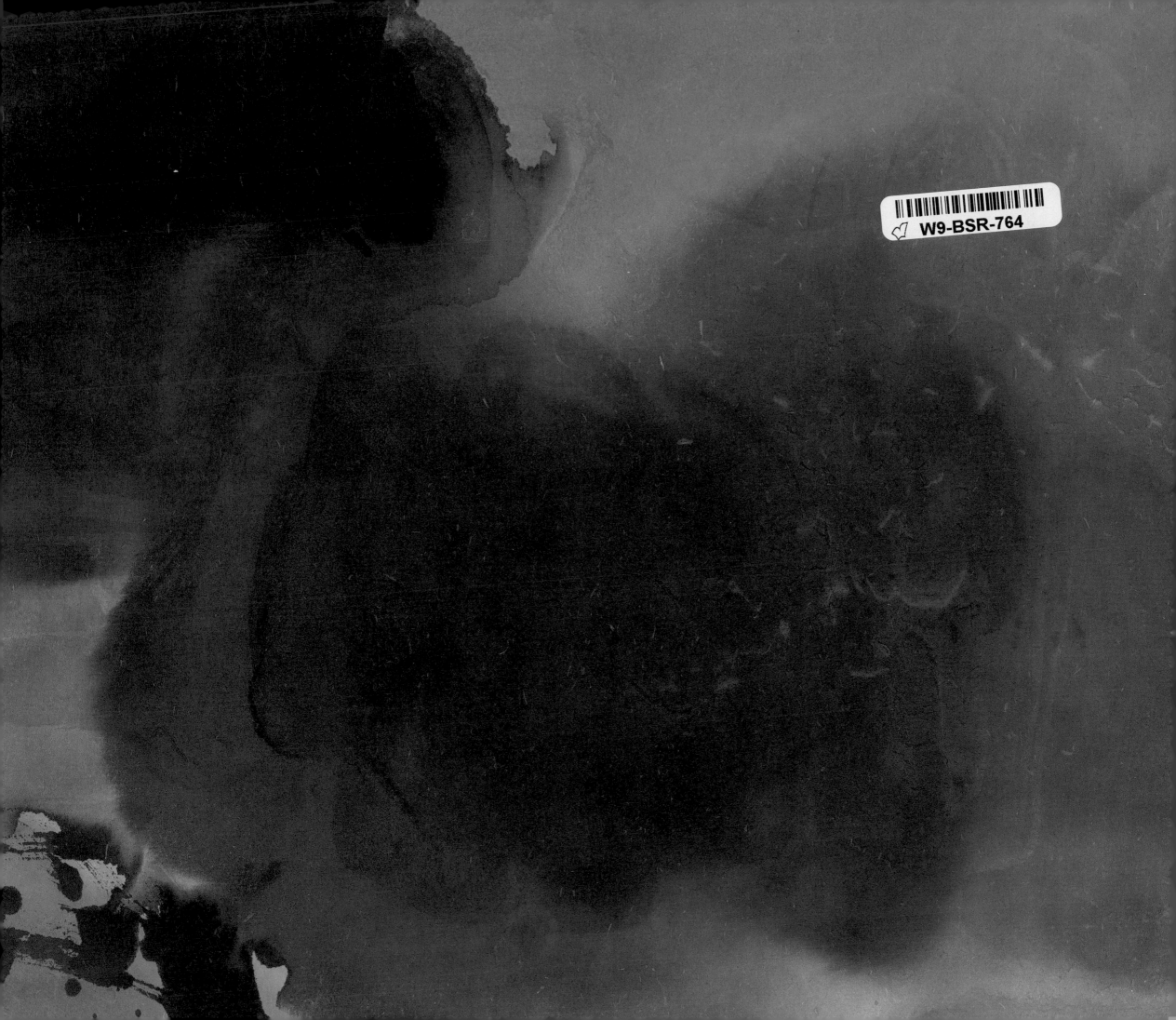

W9-BSR-764

Mr. Waldron

go steelers!

thanks for being a good teacher for me.

your friend
Jordan

your great

I will make miracles

I will make miracles

Susie Morgenstern

illustrated by Jiang Hong Chen

BLOOMSBURY
CHILDREN'S
BOOKS

Everyone keeps asking me,
When you get older, what will you be?

I say a plumber or pilot.
Or dance the ballet!

Though the truth is I don't really
know what to say.

But today I woke up and peeked out my left eye,
And the sun had just started to climb to the sky.
That's when I realized it just might be fun
To spend every morning waking the sun.

Then I might stir up the waves in the ocean.
My undersea concert would
rock with commotion!

Next thing I'd do, I'd heal all the sick
With vanilla milk shakes,
creamy and thick!

I'd wake the dead, I'd wake them all,
And give them one last chance
to play ball!

What about the bad guys?
I'd help the police.

We'd send them away
and have some peace!

I'd make the world stop fighting!
I'd get it down in writing!
I'd shout it far and near.
And everyone would hear.

I'd lock the bad guys up in cages
And turn them into wise old sages.

I'll make miracles my mission
And be the number-one magician.

I'll meet everyone on Earth,
and ask about their dreams.
Because life is more,
much more than it seems.

My giant loaf of bread will cure the world of hunger,
And people who eat it will feel ten years younger!

And then for the child who has nothing to wear,
I'll sew her a dress. That will answer her prayer.

I will stamp out earthquakes, floods, and fire—
The world will stop shaking, be cooler and drier.

I will stretch out our days and our nights to feel longer
So everyone has enough time to grow stronger.

I'll fill up the world with people who share,
With people who smile, with people who care.

It might sound like God is who I want to be—
And maybe it's true. But here is the key:

To change the world from dark to bright,
First I should learn to read and write.

Typeset in Sunshine
Art created with colored Chinese ink on rice paper

Published by Bloomsbury U.S.A. Children's Books
175 Fifth Avenue, New York, NY 10010
Distributed to the trade by Holtzbrinck Publishers

Library of Congress Cataloging-in-Publication Data
available upon request
ISBN-13: 978-1-59990-189-3 • ISBN-10: 1-59990-189-7

First U.S. Edition 2008
Printed in China
1 3 5 7 9 10 8 6 4 2